THE LONG WAY HOME

A CHRISTMAS STORY

WRITTEN AND ILLUSTRATED BY

S T E P H E N   C H A R L E S   L A   P A N T A

Stephen Charles La Panta

The approaching Christmas season is the catalyst in Michael's personal realization that he has allowed his work and his struggle for advancement to consume his life at the expense of his family.

Through a series of flashbacks of Christmas memories from his own childhood, the re-discovery of a toy train which he received on one of those Christmases and the love and support of a strong and understanding wife, he makes the journey from detached indifference to a renewed appreciation of the importance of family and the expression of love.

S T E P H E N   C H A R L E S   L A   P A N T A

Cover and Layout Design By Rhonda Ann Cronin

Text Copyright © 1995 by Stephen Charles LaPanta
Illustrations Copyright © 1996 by Stephen Charles LaPanta
The use of "LIONEL" under written license from Lionel LLC

Second Printing.
Homeward Bound Publishing, New Brighton. Minnesota.
Printed and bound in the United States of America.
Printed by Printing Enterprises INC, New Brighton, Minnesota.

To Judy Lee . . .

*For unlimited patience, unqualified support,
unwavering faith and unending love
and for helping me find my way home.*

With love and gratitude to . . .

*Anthony, Margo, Mathew, Darcy,
Amelia, Sean, Stephen Michael
and grandsons A.J. and Vincent John . . .
for providing the inspiration for my story
and the encouragement to share it
with families everywhere.*

As fall disappeared beneath a blanket of snow . . .

she watched, in silence, from her kitchen window,

sipping her morning coffee.

It was the first snowfall in early December . . .

the most beautiful that Emily could ever remember,

winter had fallen so softly.

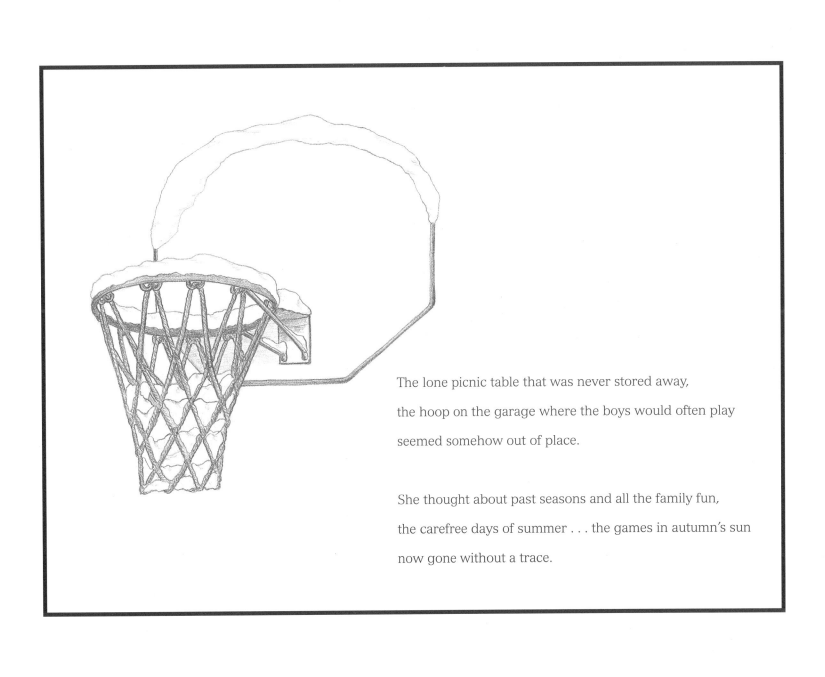

The lone picnic table that was never stored away,

the hoop on the garage where the boys would often play

seemed somehow out of place.

She thought about past seasons and all the family fun,

the carefree days of summer . . . the games in autumn's sun

now gone without a trace.

"It's hard to believe it's that time again . . .

we just get it all packed away and then

another year has passed."

Michael bemoaned the task at hand,

the boxes of lights . . . the old tree stand

stored since Christmas last.

"There must be a dozen boxes up here . . .

twice as many as there were last year,"

he complained from the attic door.

"With all that I have going on right now

I frankly can't even imagine how

you think I have time for more.

Why couldn't you and the kids handle this?

I can't understand why you always insist

on making a major production.

I should probably be at the office today . . .

if I'm there by myself, there's a good chance I may

get some work done without interruption."

Emily called up from the hallway below . . .

"If that's how you feel, Michael, climb down and go.

You're really not here anyway.

Do you think you'll have time for us Christmas Eve . . .

or will work be so pressing, that you'll have to leave . . .

and can we plan on you Christmas day?"

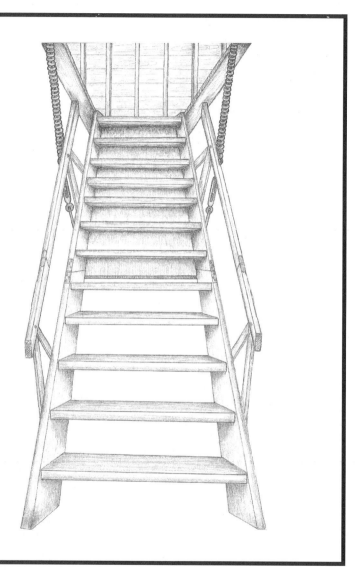

"It's no joke," he said tersely, descending the stair . . .

"corporate called Friday . . . our sales don't compare

through the month of November last year.

I still have a couple of big projects pending,

and if I complete them before the year ending . . .

it would probably help my career."

Though aware of the pressure that Michael was under . . .

Emily was feeling their lives torn asunder

by forces beyond her control.

Slowly at first . . . he seemed ever more distant,

in family matters, he was almost indifferent . . .

his work was taking its toll.

"Michael, I don't like what's happened to us!

When I try to approach you with plans to discuss,

you rarely have time anymore.

Your job is important, as well it should be . . .

but you've also a place in your own family

which you cannot choose to ignore.

We can't celebrate Christmas . . . schedule permitting,

our lives can't be put on hold at your bidding . . .

the children and I need you now."

Though her words struck a chord . . . there was no time for reason

he wanted to balance his work and the season . . .

but sadly, he didn't know how.

As he picked up his briefcase and started to leave,

he felt his small daughter's tug at his sleeve . . .

he turned to see she was crying.

"Daddy, what about Christmas?" she asked through her tears,

"and Santa, and Rudolph and all the reindeer?"

Michael knew there would be no denying.

As he bent to one knee on the foyer rug,

he said,"Come here sweetheart, and give Daddy a hug."

She jumped to his outstretched arms.

Despite all his worries . . . he was utterly beguiled

by the wide-eyed innocence of his youngest child

and all her little girl charms.

"I know that I promised," he began to explain . . .

but the tears in her eyes made him feel the pain

that his work was causing his family.

It was difficult for her to understand why . . .

impossible for him to somehow justify

a need only he could see.

"I'm sure Daddy wishes he didn't have to go,"

Emily said in support . . . it was small comfort though

to a child whose heart was breaking.

Watching from the window as he disappeared from sight,

she assured the children, "Everything is all right . . ."

while inside, her own heart was aching.

Shopkeepers were trimming their windows with care,

while garland was hung from the clock in the square . . .

the streets were alive with Christmas.

Michael paid no attention as he hurried by,

he had some new concepts he was eager to try . . .

and his thoughts were filled with his business.

He sat down at his computer in mid-afternoon

having promised his children he would be home soon

to help with the Christmas tree.

His work went so smoothly that in no time at all

he took a short break to give Emily a call

to tell her what time he'd be free.

Leaning back in his chair he picked up the phone,

but just as he started to dial his home . . .

Michael paused when he noticed the time.

He had worked through the day and into the night,

he looked at his watch, the desk clock was right . . .

waves of guilt crossed his troubled mind.

He thought of his family waiting alone . . .

the patience and understanding they'd shown,

when he told them he couldn't stay.

Now it was almost quarter to twelve . . .

they probably put the tree up themselves,

after waiting most of the day.

As his car pushed its way through the new fallen snow,

the cold evening air seemed warmed by the glow

of the beautiful lights of Christmas.

He remembered how excited he and Maggie had been,

every year when the crews put the lights up again . . .

it was time to make out their wish list.

A two wheel bike . . . an electric train,

a first baseman's glove, a Monopoly® game . . .

then Dad said they had to choose one.

Waiting in line at the department store . . .

they anxiously reviewed their choices once more

then Santa said, "Step up here son . . .

Why don't you stand right here next to me

and I'll lift your sister up on my knee . . .

Now then, what would you like me to bring?"

Reflected in the face of himself as a boy,

Michael saw the same sparkle of wonder and joy

in his small daughter's eyes that morning.

It seems as though it could have been yesterday . . .

Michael thought to himself, as he made his way

through the streets of his hometown.

Pulling into the driveway of his boyhood home,

he was reminded of Christmases he had known . . .

with his family and friends all around.

For there in the window . . . silent vigil in the night,

stood a beautiful tree with lights burning bright . . .

Michael's memory stirred once more . . .

To when he and Maggie would walk home from skating,

and Mom would have cookies and hot cocoa waiting

as soon as they came in the door.

It seemed that everything was simpler then . . . life was carefree and secure

and Mom and Dad were always there to love and reassure

his was truly a wonderful childhood.

He recalled how excitement filled the house this time each year,

when family members traveled home as Christmas Eve drew near . . .

he tried to wait up as late as he could.

He smiled, remembering how the whole family

would have to agree on the choice of a tree,

before Dad tied it on the car.

And carefully unpacking antique decorations

which had been in the family for generations

to find the cherished old star.

Decorating the tree was especially exciting.

Dad would darken the room and countdown to lighting,

then everyone would cheer.

Returning from his peaceful reverie . . .

Michael came face to face with the harsh reality

that was all too painfully clear.

His commitment to work had gone out of control

he had sacrificed everything, body and soul,

including his own family.

They had asked for so little . . . he gave even less

he became so focused on achieving success

that soon he was too blind to see.

He thought about all of the promises broken

the deep disappointments . . . the anger unspoken

when he let them down time after time.

He saw Emily alone at a party or concert

explaining his absence, while hiding her own hurt . . .

bravely saying, "I really don't mind."

He envisioned his children . . . justifiably proud

at a game or recital . . . eyes scanning the crowd . . .

then discovering he wasn't there.

Michael questioned the motive for all that he'd done

and the husband and father that he had become . . .

slowly climbing the front porch stair.

With a heart full of sadness . . . his spirits were low

the small family dog seemed somehow to know,

as he tried to welcome him home.

Following the gentle harmony of a Christmas choir,

he found Emily sleeping by an amber fire . . .

waiting patiently near the phone.

Noticing the tissues in her hand and on the floor . . .

Michael knew she had been crying and he could not ignore

the fact that he was the reason why.

As he looked around the room at all the work that had been done,

he felt guilty when he thought of how he'd failed to be the one

upon whom she could rely.

Emily's touch was everywhere and it warmed his heart to see

how she had recreated Christmas . . . so painstakingly

in spite of life's demands.

The counted cross-stitched stockings . . . the Santas on the mantel,

the beautiful nativity . . . the potpourri and candles,

all placed with loving hands.

Stepping over boxes on his way to tend the fire . . .

Michael paused by the boughs of the tree to admire

the family ornament collection.

Displayed among the crafted works of porcelain and glass

were the treasures that the children made for scouting or in class,

hanging proudly for inspection.

He smiled, recalling how each child had come home
with their special creation . . . glued, painted or sewn . . .
to add to the Christmas tree.

And the pride and excitement on each little face,
as they were encouraged to choose just the right place
to hang it where all would see.

Turning to the hearth in the flickering light . . .

his eye caught a glimpse of a long-forgotten sight,

a box he thought he recognized.

Upon taking a closer look . . . he remembered it well

it was a blue and orange box with the name, "Lionel®,"

emblazoned on the top and on the sides.

When Emily had instructed the boys to bring down

all of the boxes marked "Christmas" they found . . .

there were several from Christmases past.

And a childhood memory which Michael held dear

that must have been stored in the attic for years

was now rediscovered at last.

The colors were faded . . . the edges were worn

some tape had been placed where the corners were torn

but, to him it was as if it were new.

It was Christmas morning as he watched a small boy . . .

slip off the cover . . . his heart filled with joy

for a Christmas wish come true.

And there in the compartments of the box before him lay

the cars, caboose and engines of the mighty Santa Fe . . .

replicas in perfect scale.

It was exactly what he had asked Santa to bring

a model railroad . . . just like the real thing

authentic in every detail!

Now as Michael opened the box once more . . .

he relived the excitement of thirty years before

on that memorable Christmas day.

He touched each car just as he did then . . .

and held the silver diesel with its red and yellow trim,

the centerpiece of the display.

He recalled how his father had spread the parts out on the floor

carefully reading the instructions . . . to learn what each was for,

before starting to put them together.

He cautioned, "Michael, you mustn't think of your new train as a toy,

but rather, as a hobby, to be respected and enjoyed . . .

this you must always remember."

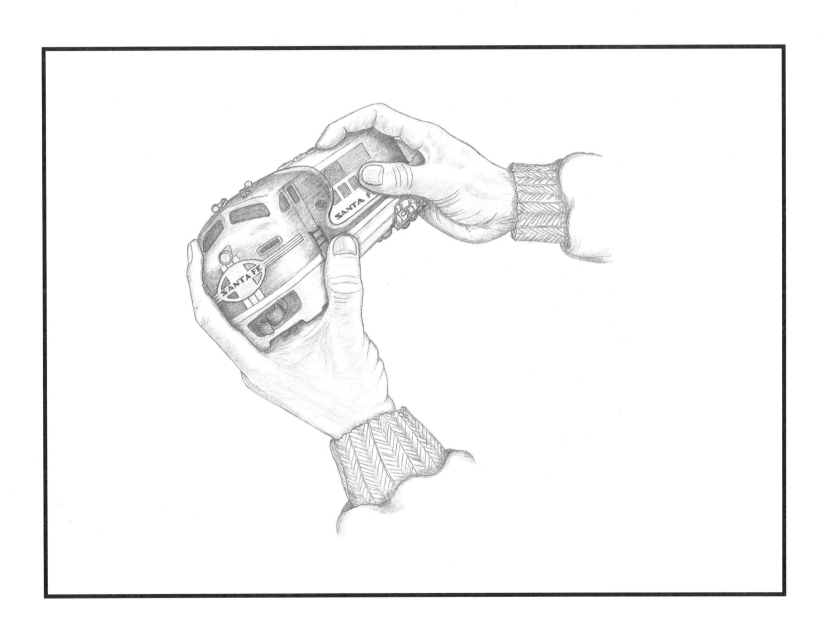

Michael felt his father's hand guiding his upon the throttle.

He remembered laughing nervously as he watched the life-like model

seeming to move on its own.

They raced along the straight-aways . . . then slowed down through the turns

his father gradually eased his grip as Michael began to learn . . .

soon he was running his train alone.

"You're on your own now, Michael . . . you know what to do

you're handling it like a big boy, son . . . I'm very proud of you."

The words still echoed in his mind.

He wondered how long it had been . . . if ever

that his children had heard that from him . . . maybe never,

he had given them so little time.

He had counted on Emily to be mother and father

and though they both worked . . . he never thought her

career as important as his.

In his own mind he had found ways to justify

the fact that he was too busy to even try

to be there for her and the kids.

Without ever making a conscious choice

or allowing his family to have a voice,

he had simply gone his own way.

"It's not just for me . . . I'm doing this for you

it's part of my job . . . it's what I must do."

Michael could hear himself say.

Now as he looked at her lying there . . .

he thought of the special times they used to share,

and he felt ashamed at the sight.

Kneeling down by the couch where Emily was sleeping

he whispered aloud, "Thank you for keeping

my promise to the children tonight."

He kissed her gently and as she started to wake

he said, "Please forgive me, honey . . . I'm sorry I'm late

though I don't deserve it, please try."

She reached up . . . and touching the side of his face . . .

brought her fingers across his lips in a trace

then brushed a small tear from her eye.

She said, "I understand, Michael . . . really, I do

but the kids are growing older . . . we are too

and time has changed us in so many ways.

I cherish the family times we've shared together

and I'm saddened when I think that maybe we'll never

recapture the joy of those days."

"Please let me try," he said softly, while stroking her hair.

"I can't explain why I've been so unaware

of all you were handling alone."

Honey, all I can say is . . . "I apologize,

I wouldn't think of trying to rationalize

the lack of attention I've shown.

I wish that I could somehow right mistakes that I have made,

and regain a portion of the precious price already paid

but time lost is gone forever."

She said, "Michael, let's forget the past . . . and any pain and sorrow."

And with her arms around him said, "Let's think about tomorrow

and the family we share together."

Then noticing the box she asked, "Is that your old toy train?"

"It's my hobby!" he corrected, then smiling . . . he explained

the lesson his father had taught him.

He told her of the boyhood wish he'd made on Santa's knee . . .

and the thrill he felt on Christmas day when there beneath the tree

lay the gift that Santa had brought him.

"I had forgotten how it felt to be a child at Christmas time . . .

but I've come the long way home tonight . . . through the memories of my mind . . .

and I don't want the journey to end."

Emily took his hand in hers . . . and in the glow of the Christmas tree,

they sat down by the fire and talked of what had come to be,

each one listening once again.

They talked of happy memories . . . their dreams . . . and their fears,

openly and honestly for the first time in years

until the darkness became a new day.

Soon they heard the children stirring in the bedrooms up the stairs

then a sleepy little angel with a well-worn teddy bear

shyly peeked in from the hallway.

"Daddy's home!" she cried out as she ran across the room.

The others scrambled out of bed . . . rushed downstairs . . . and soon

were clamoring for Michael's attention.

"Did you see we put the tree up, Dad? . . . Do you think we did it right?

Doesn't the tinsel look pretty? . . . Did we do a good job with the lights?"

Each was vying to ask him a question.

"It's the most beautiful tree in the world." Michael said with tears in his eyes.

Then gathering his children around him he said, "Thanks for the perfect surprise,

I'm so proud of all of you!"

His little daughter questioned, "Why does Christmas make you sad?"

"My tears are tears of joy, sweetheart, for the blessings that I have . . .

and I've been given quite a few."

"What's a blessing, Daddy?" she asked persistently,

"and since you have so many . . . will you share some with me?"

Michael smiled through his tears . . .

He said, "A blessing is a special gift that comes from God alone . . .

it's parents, and children, the happiness in our home,

and all that we hold dear . . .

It's brothers, and sisters, and grandmas and grandpas too,

it's the friendship that you share with all those close to you . . .

but most of all . . . it's love.

The love of friends and family that touches us each day,

the calming love that surrounds us when we kneel in faith to pray

for guidance from above.

Can you share my blessings with me? I guess I thought you knew.

You are my special blessings and I thank God for all of you

and I love you with all my heart.

But I took my blessings for granted, thinking you would always be there,

whenever I could get caught up and have some time to spare.

Now I need to make a new start.

You see, last night I met an old friend and he reminded me,

that of all the Christmas gifts we give, the most cherished one would be . . .

the time we spend together.

So my special gift this Christmas and each day throughout the year . . .

is my promise that when you need me, I will always be here

because a family is forever."

Then peering in the box, his oldest son exclaimed . . .

"Hey come and look at this . . . it's a real old-fashioned train."

Michael smiled and winked at Emily.

"It was a morning much like this one when I first saw my train . . .

though I was just about your age, the feelings still remain

a vivid childhood memory.

Your Aunt Maggie and I would spend hours lying on the bedroom floor,

watching the train circle under the bed and across to the chest of drawers . . .

in our world of make believe.

And soon it was part of our family tradition,

that it wouldn't be Christmas without the addition . . .

of the train circling under the tree."

The children asked, "How come Aunt Maggie never comes to see us anymore?"

Michael realized at once that it was he who closed the door . . .

recalling her last invitation . . .

"Thanks for the invite . . . but we'll have to pass,

I can't get away now . . . " he wrote in his fax

offering no further explanation.

"You know, Michael," said Emily, "perhaps it's a sign . . .

we have plenty of room . . . and I think it's time . . . "

Michael went straight to the phone.

"We would love to come, Michael . . . of course . . . but I thought . . ."

"Please, Maggie!" he pleaded, "it would mean a lot

to have the whole family back home.

I think that we all have some catching up to do . . .

neglected relationships we must renew . . .

and our children should know one another.

We've made some mistakes, no one knows more than I

but if you are willing to give it a try . . .

I'd still like to be your big brother."

Preparations were frantic . . . so much to be done

cleaning and baking . . . where to put everyone?

They'd arrive the day after tomorrow.

Shopping and wrapping . . . and presents to label,

two extra leaves for the dining room table . . .

and still three more chairs yet to borrow.

The yule log was burning . . . the candles were lighted,

the tree was aglow, everyone was excited

and rich Christmas scents filled the air.

"They're here! They're here!" the children exclaimed.

Michael called, "Merry Christmas! We're so glad you came!

We've a wonderful season to share!"

And all at once the differences that had deepened over time . . .

through the healing of forgiving hearts . . . disappeared from mind

amid tearful warm embraces.

Michael reached for Maggie's hand and said, "There's something you must see . . .

it's a treasure from our childhood rediscovered recently . . .

some memories time never erases."

Then signaling his children . . . the lights were turned down low

and as they stood together in the Christmas tree's warm glow,

childhood memories began to take flight.

When out of the darkness, a train's whistle sounded

and a single headlight lit the way as it rounded

the turn and came into sight.

"The Santa Fe!" she whispered in tearful disbelief,

as Christmas past returned aboard the ageless Super Chief . . .

They were children once again.

And magically, the warmth and love of Christmas memories

touched their hearts and those of their extended families,

as they talked of what had been.

They reminisced of childhood dreams and growing up together

and how, as children, they had thought those days would last forever,

always family . . . best of friends.

Now with children of their own, they realized that it was true,

if we hold the magic in our hearts each day the whole year through . . .

the spirit of Christmas never ends.

Now everyone was home again, as it was meant to be,

a family reunited, in peace and harmony . . .

sharing love and laughter.

As he looked around the room . . . Michael knew deep in his heart,

that family time together would always be a special part

of Christmas ever after.

At dinnertime, when all joined hands and bowed their heads to pray . . .

he gave thanks for all life's blessings and the most wonderful Christmas day

that he had ever known.

And when his prayer was ended and the Christmas cheer began,

Emily leaned toward Michael . . . gently squeezed his hand

and whispered . . . *"Welcome home!"*